It's A Marshmallow World

DIANE RINELLA

For the real Darla.

Acknowledgements

Fate is a funny thing. One day, Joanne Brothwell, an author whom I had admired for quite some time, awarded a few of her favorite new releases as prizes in a Christmas contest. One of those books was a copy of my first novel, *Love's Forbidden Flower*. Some chick named Darla won. I took a moment to hope she would like it, and then went back to my Christmas shopping.

A few days later, that same chick sent me a Facebook friend request. Could it be that I had a fan? How cool!

Since then, Darla Roybal has become my stalker in the most wonderful sense of the word. She is the fan that every author dreams of—friendly, supportive, laughter-inducing, and inspiring. Somewhere along the line I got even luckier, and she became my dear friend.

Darla also (in her wonderful, charming, stalker way) harassed me about naming a character Darla. The character didn't have to be anything like her, but the name did matter. (Okay, it wasn't truly harassment, but more of a mischievous hint at something she thought would never happen.) When *Scary Modsters* was released, she got her wish in the form of a minor character with a wacky sense of humor, questionable taste in music, and hair that shares the same colors as peacock feathers. But the laugh was on me. While I had fun with the little, be-careful-what-you-wish-for joke, so many people fell in love with fake Darla that it was obvious she needed a tale all her own. I now give you Darla's story—a stand-alone, prequel to *Scary Modsters*.

But before I do that …

Every author has a few special ingredients that make her work complete. I owe many of my lovely covers, including this one, to artist Heidi "Azurylipfe" Darras. Together, we make magic.

Parade Of The Wooden Soldiers

Christmas Day, 2000

Darla

For seventeen years, Christmas mornings have left me crawling through mounds of Santa-covered paper, knowing that somewhere under the rubble lay my gifts. My family doesn't know when to stop buying. That is, except for Dad. Once he buys Mom jewelry and a couple of gift cards, all there is left for him to do is sneak cookies out of the freezer. He's the sane one.

Mom is always at such a loss for Dad's gifts that November first has become Day of the Dread. By that morning, she had better come up with an idea for his present, because it is either spend a month and a half hunting it down on eBay or succumbing to evil, going to Amazon, and clicking her index finger into traction.

For Dad's grandma, we head to Claire's and The Gap. Mom stocks her up on sweaters while Bailey and I buy her the latest accessories. GranGran is the wildest person I know. Getting her something "suitable" for a woman of her age would be an insult not only to her, but also to all those who live without restrictions. She rules!

Bailey and I spare Mom agony by making our wish lists before we decide on our Halloween costumes. Within reason, Mom's itchy trigger finger clicks us whatever we want. She then wraps everything individually—hence the avalanche.

Bailey reaches under the tree, and I can't help but be jealous of her new hair color. It looks black, but in the right light it is deep purple. First I am going to win the battle with wearing makeup my way, then I will tackle dying my hair. Somehow it will happen, and I won't have to wait until I turn eighteen next year like Dad says.

Bailey hands me a present about the size of a shoebox but twice as tall. The motion causes something inside it to shift. It's got some weight to it. I give it a little shake. It seems like there are a lot of little things sliding around. Could it be?

Oh please!

Oh please! Oh please! Oh please!

My hands tear at the paper, yet when it comes time to open the box I exercise caution. My tilted head and squinted eyes project my thought of *"I don't know if I trust you."*

The sparkle in Bailey's chocolate eyes is as bright as her laughter. "Yeah, Darla, I'd wonder about anything coming from me, too."

Inside is a makeup case—a cute, scaled down version of what the pros use. My heart starts skipping all over the place. Although Dad has really tried to keep his cool about him, ever since my boobs started growing faster than the rest of me, he has been in panic mode. As a result, the only colors I've been able to get away with adding to my face are twenty shades of drab. I'm so tired of blending in with the wallpaper. It's time to bloom!

The *click* of unsnapping the locks sends a wave of hope through my stomach.

Bummer. The contents bring about a reserved smile. It contains some lipstick, mascara, an eyeliner pencil, and an eyeshadow palette with colors that are only a step above boring. But hey, this is better than the stuff I already have.

Now that Mom and Dad have turned to check on GranGran, Bailey clears her throat and then nudges her head towards the bottom of the box.

The outside looks like the inside should be deeper than it is. Actually, the inside bottom looks unstable, and the fabric doesn't quite match that on the sides.

I dig at the corner and have to fight off my gasp when I

see container upon container of professional-quality eyeshadow forming a rainbow of delight. Tucked into the corners are tubes of lipsticks. The one I slip a peek at is bright, nearly neon, pink. This rules! Bailey has hooked me up, epically!

How did Bailey afford all of this? Mom and Dad always finance our gifts to each other, but this one is a little heavy handed.

Mom is peeking over her shoulder. I see what is really happening here. She thinks she is being sly. If this comes from Bailey, Dad can't get angry at her. That's why she tossed me extra money to buy my sister something special. I thought it was because Bailey plans to move out soon. While that may have something to do with it, Mom is trying to hide the real agenda.

Dad turns his head, and I race to conceal the rainbow. He snickers before turning away.

Snickers? Dad is snickering?

He knows!

Does Mom know he knows?

He turns back with wide eyes and rattles his head, warning me not to say a word. Oh yeah, he knows all right, and he is having fun by letting everyone think they are pulling the wool over his eyes. My family is wacky.

Bailey eyes Mom and Dad. She sees through the act as much as I do. "That comes with makeup lessons, too," she says. Sweet! Bailey is studying to be a professional makeup artist. Those lessons may be the main reason why this gift has been parentally approved.

I thank her, profusely. Oh my God, Rox and Jacqueline are going to be so jealous! They may be the sweetest friends in the universe, but they are hard to stand next to. Rox always looks so funky and fun, while Jacqueline could wear mud and look perfect. I can't wait for them to get a load of me with some of this on!

Out of the corner of my eye, I catch GranGran smiling. Her too? Well, duh! Of course her too. She was probably the mastermind that got everyone on board with this. I race over to show her the goods—the bright and sparkly stuff that is tucked away. She kisses my head. "Awesome!" She then whispers, "I am totally jealous." By the way her eyes twinkle, I believe her. She and I are the only ones in the family with green eyes. The more time that passes, the more I see that genetic traits are not all that I have gotten from her. Being like her is an honor.

I bend in and whisper, "I know that somehow you had a hand in this. Thank you."

She winks.

Yeah, I thought so.

After getting this haul, now I really can't wait to give Bailey her gift. I hand her what is obviously a wooden, crate-type box wrapped in Christmas paper. She rips the paper away to find a set of four, small bottles of flavored, balsamic vinegars. The look on her face is priceless. She is too gracious to ask what is up, even though she has got to know there is a joke behind this.

"Thank you. I've wanted to experiment with cooking more." It takes all I have not to laugh until reality strikes her. "Wait a minute. This crate has been messed with. Why are the seals around the necks of the bottles removed? And why is it that even though some of these say they are flavored things that should be dark, all of the fluids are colorless?"

"Maybe you should open them and find out."

She unscrews a cap and raises the bottle towards her nose. Hesitantly, she inhales. "Intensity," I say.

She gasps. "No!"

"Keep going." She pulls out another bottle and goes in to smell. "Scentimental Journey," I tell her.

"No way! You bought me the perfumes I've been wanting? This is incredible."

"It was kind of amazing that with all the cool perfume bottles out there, the ones for those were boring. Plus, even though I don't want to admit it, we all know you are dying to move out of the house. If every morning you look on your vanity and see vinegar bottles, you won't forget the sister you left all alone and wallowing in misery."

Bailey races over to give me a hug that nearly knocks me onto my back. "I love how you never do anything like a normal person would."

Her words make my heart sing. I can't think of a fate worse than being boring.

GranGran's semi-bouffant bops as she tosses her hands in the air. "Finally, it's my turn!" Her youthfulness always seems to amaze everyone but me. Her cane may not suit her personality, but the red highlights that cover the signs of aging seem as natural on her as they would on a woman a quarter of her age. She's not some elderly great grandmother; she's GranGran—a force all her own.

She hands Bailey and I boxes that are tightly wrapped in red, metallic paper and green ribbon that cascades over the edges. Bailey and I exchange smiles. Gifts from GranGran are always sweet and sentimental. We look forward to them more than anything else on Christmas morning; that is, with the exception of what she gives us later in private.

Bailey and I open our presents in unison, both stopping at the sight of something precious. This year GranGran has given us treasured memories preserved on paper—photos of us taken with her on Thanksgiving. The frames are perfect— red and white cloisonné roses for Bailey—pink and yellow daisies for me. The frame reminds me of the hair clips she gave me for my sixteenth birthday. I love those so much that I fear losing them and only pull them out for special occasions. Daisies are so beautiful. I love how they burst with life and—

A chill travels up my spine, as if words of horror were whispered in my ear. There is something eerie about this photo. I can't quite place it but …

The dining room chandelier is in the background, just below GranGran's head. The glow of its lights reminds me of a halo. My stomach squeezes. Never before have I thought of GranGran as being mortal. My distorted perception has told me she will always be around. Suddenly reality is swooping in. Eventually life ends for all of us. It is inevitable.

"Something to always remember our good times by," she says.

GranGran's words strike a chord of sorrow, driving home what my heart is telling me. She knows something. Now I do, too. Judging by the hollowness in Bailey's eyes, I see that she senses it as well.

Bailey and I dash to hug her. My words choke out. "I absolutely love it. Thank you, GranGran."

I am so grateful that she is here. I pray that I live to be ninety-two years old, and that I do it in the health and style that she has. She is a woman who loves life—a woman who evolves. When she was born, people scarcely had electricity in their homes. Now she is so in love with technology that she bought Bailey and I cell phones with texting plans so we can share our whims. All of my friends are jealous that I have my own cell phone, and while that is awesome, it is not what matters.

I kiss her cheek, take her hands in mine, and lock eyes with her. My tears flow with the pride of being her descendant. In light of my revelation, fear makes it hard to keep my words steady. "Thank you, GranGran. You are always the best Christmas present I could ever get."

Lord, please let me be wrong. Please bless us with more Christmases together.

Once the official festivities are over, my favorite part of Christmas arrives. Bailey and I each go to our rooms so that GranGran can give us what she considers to be our real Christmas presents. The gift is secondary to how much we cherish this time with her—a time to tell stories, share secrets, and to just be girls.

Laughter travels through the wall of Bailey's room and in to mine. Knowing those two, I'll bet dollars to doughnuts that GranGran is telling war stories again. Not just war time stories, but stories about the men she met during World War II—ones who figured a daring advance on a lady was far less dangerous than what they would soon face on a battlefield. Bailey is fascinated with old movies, Big Band Jazz, Swing dancing, and vintage fashions. Her makeup collection is filled with compacts and lipstick cases that date back to the nineteen thirties and forties, all thanks to GranGran's love of eBay.

The laughter subsides, and Bailey's door closes. Feet, aided by a tapping cane, shuffle down the hall. I surprise GranGran by answering before she can knock. We both laugh. "My gosh," she says. Her hand flies to her heart like I've shocked her. It nearly causes her to drop the long, short box that is tucked under her arm. "You darn near gave me a heart attack. Remember, people claim that at my age I am a little on the fragile side." She rolls her eyes.

"Yeah, right. If there is one thing I know, it is that you are anything but fragile."

She shakes her cane at me. "I'm the toughest weed in the garden, and don't you ever forget it! Life has dealt me so much that I've become immune to weed killer."

Something about her smile says she is telling tales. There is a wobble to her step that didn't exist at Thanksgiving, and it brings back the ache my heart felt when I opened the picture.

She drops onto my bed and pats for me to sit. "You are in trouble."

I plop down next to her while not buying into her firm tone for a second. "Why?" I ask, although I suspect I know the answer. I just want the whole mess to go away.

"I'll give you a hint. Today is Monday. That means I've been waiting *three whole days!*"

I groan and drop my head. Busted.

"I've talked to you twice since Friday, and not once have you filled me in on what happened. I know that had it been great, you would have told me. If it had been truly bad, you would have been on my doorstep. Silence leaves me to believe that the event didn't lead to another date, the loss of your virginity, or police involvement."

Lord! Again she is my freaking mind reader. "You're right! I should have told you. If it makes you feel any better, I haven't filled in anyone but Bailey, and that was purely out of necessity."

GranGran raises her brow. "Oh, this sounds bad. Not even Rox or Jacqueline?"

Time to blurt it out so she can stop worrying. "No, and as I am sure you can tell, I am fine. The real reason that jerk asked me to the Winter Ball was so he could spy on his bimbo ex."

"Oh, that bites," she says.

"No kidding!"

GranGran leans back and sizes me up. "There's more."

Gah! I'd ask how she knows, but we can't seem to keep secrets from each other. Why won't that night go away?

Oh shoot, as much as this sucks to admit, she'll get a kick out of it. I really had planned on telling her the next morning, but my frustration got the best of me. "Long story short, it takes a lot of balls to ignore your date the entire time, and then expect her to spend time alone with you in an empty parking lot."

She rolls her head back. "Oh, I'm betting this one has a doozy of an ending."

"I spike-heeled him in the junk, and then called Bailey to come get me."

GranGran smacks her cane on the floor. Her laugh sounds like a howl. "Oh, that is my girl! You've been raised right!" The cane gets tossed aside, and she applauds. I respond by standing to take a bow. The howls lead to a catcall. She then wipes a tear away before the laughter ends. As soon as I take back my seat next to her, she gets serious. "You okay now?"

I wave my hand at the situation. "Yeah, I always have been. Admitting I was used sucks though."

Her hand lands firmly on my knee. "Trust me darling, someday it is going to work out. Not all men are jerks, although sometimes it sure seems that way. You just keep being who you are. The right man will respect that more than you can imagine. Are you sure you are okay?"

I grumble. "Yeah, the only thing bruised is my ego. I hate when people play mind games."

"Me too, and I am glad you are smart enough not to get trapped into one. Okay, you are forgiven for not calling. Here." The box she places on my lap reminds me of a board game. Boy, wouldn't it be funny timing if she gave me a copy of the game of Life? Everything she does has meaning of some sort. Right now, that would be a hell of a metaphor.

"Thank you." I kiss her cheek and start opening the gift. She stops me.

"Darla, you know that I never play favorites with you and Bailey. You are both unique individuals and deserve to be treated as such." GranGran softens her voice. Her words seem to massage their way into me. "Although I know you will figure this out on your own, the gifts you and Bailey are getting are not only different in nature, but also in monetary value. However, the emotional value is just as great. I hope you will see that this says more about you as a person, and what you will need in the future, than anything else. Do you understand that?"

Wow. She has never thought I would be concerned over money before. Cosmetology school is just the tip of the iceberg for Bailey. She has big dreams. GranGran must be doing something to help her. I think that is great. I wish I had career direction like Bailey does. "Of course I do. You are the one who taught me that things are just things unless sentiment makes them special."

She pats my hand and nods toward the gift. "Go on. Open it."

I rip away the sparkling images of snowmen while keeping my eyes locked on the box underneath. Quickly the contents become clear. It is a board game all right—or though some claim. "A Ouija board! Wow! Really?"

GranGran laughs.

The plastic has already been removed. Maybe the box is a

9

joke. I kind of hope not. I've always wanted one of these.

I whip the lid off as if it were light as air. Just as swiftly, a wave of energy tumbles over me and clogs my thoughts. I shake my head, but I still feel kind of hazy. Am I imagining this?

I put one hand on the bed to steady myself, and eventually the fog lifts. Something definitely washed over me.

Inside the box is not only a Ouija board and planchette, but also another present wrapped in blue, metallic paper. A sticker of a daisy sits in place of a bow. When I reach for the second gift, the sensation hits again.

Did that energy come off of the board or the second gift? The board feels like it is glowing, yet I can't see the light.

Another odd vibration creeps its way into me. It is a sense of protection, like a tiger has just run out to save me from a lion. It captures a bit of my breath. There is more here than meets the eye.

With the touch of her hand, GranGran stops me from opening the package inside. "Save that gift for another day. Remember, this board is not a toy. You'll know when the time is right to explore its power." Now the glow I feel is coming off of her. It seeps into my spirit, yet I still can't take my eyes off of the second gift. Her next words hit my soul so hard, I'm uncertain if they come from her lips or are said by a voice from beyond. "You are a very special girl, Darla. No matter what you do or where you go, carry me with you." She looks away and swallows hard. Her tone and volume shift. "Well, it is getting late. These eyes don't like me driving in the dark."

"GranGran, did you do something to this? It feels … magical."

I turn to her, expecting to see the woman I've admired for so long, but something isn't right. Though a smile is still on her face, the happiness that shines ever-presently has faded. The crackle in her voice makes me feel she wants me to hear the words she is not saying more than the ones she is. "Darling Darla, everything we share is magical." Water builds in her eyes, and her lower lip slightly quivers. Loss is coming.

I've been feeling it, and now I am seeing it. God, I have to be wrong. "GranGran, are you okay?"

Like a snap, she perks up. "Come on. See me to the door."

"GranGran?"

Her rise from the bed is slow yet steady, thanks to the assistance of her cane. I stand to help her, but she waves me off. "I'm fine, dear. Arthritis ain't got nothing on me."

I touch her arm to stop her. "GranGran?" She keeps trudging ahead like she doesn't hear me. My heart breaks not only over what is happening, but also how she won't let us face it together.

Finally she stops and turns to me. Though her voice is now steady, her eyes weep. "Never, ever, let the circumstances of your body dictate the health of your spirit." She continues to move on. Just outside my door, she calls to the family that it is getting dark and she needs to go.

By the time we all see her to the porch, she seems normal as can be. When she kisses me goodbye, she leans in and whispers, "I told your sister to forget about her gift until it is absolutely needed. Bailey will need to lose her way to come home again. Be there for her when that happens. Meanwhile, remember all the things I have given you, and never hesitate to use them. Above all, always follow the daisies."

Follow the daisies?

Before I can ask, she touches a finger to my lips, encouraging my silence. Although I watch Dad walk her to the car, I feel as if she has slipped away into nothing.

"What did you get?" Bailey asks. Her voice sounds as solemn as my heart feels.

"Moments that will last a lifetime. You?"

"The same, plus a modest savings bond. GranGran has never given me money before. Why would she now?"

My spine shudders, causing me to draw in the winter air that chills my lungs. Bailey and I turn to each other and find we share the same wide-eyed looks of concern. We bolt out the door, down the driveway, and stop GranGran from entering the car for one more hug. "I love you, GranGran."

"And I you, dear. Remember, follow those daisies."

She drives off into the sun that sets before her. My heart continues to ache, yet I can't lose sight of her smile, her laugh, and the warmth she brings. Although I know there is something I am missing in its meaning, one thing is certain; between Bailey and I, I got the better gift.

January 8, 2001

I gasp, completely flabbergasted by my reflection. "Oh my …

"Oh my God.

"This is perfect! Absolutely perfect!"

Like a magician waving a wand, Bailey has turned a mirror in front of me. After a week of experiments that have left me unsatisfied, I can't believe what I see is real. I look so cool yet so elegant. If I saw me on the street, I would not know if I was going to a swanky, fifties cocktail party or if I am headed for a club. This makeup is so colorful, yet it's not all that bright. It is nothing like I would've done, but I absolutely love it! "How did you come up with this idea?" I ask Bailey.

"I finally caught on to the obvious. Dad would freak if I did too much, so I pulled an Elizabeth Taylor. You two have a similar complexion and softness to your features. She never looked overdone, even though her eyelids were heavy and her lips were bright red. The big difference is that I worked off of your green eyes with the shadowing. The base has Forest with a hint of bright green in the corners to make them pop. I also went for a brighter, pink lipstick than most women would wear."

She hands me a tube of lip gloss. The glitter in it makes me swoon. "Knowing you," she continues, "it was hard not to add this, but that would have been a little much. Save it for later. If people give you a bad time, I am sure you will want to fuel the fire. This would really give them something to talk about."

I laugh, partially because she is right and partially because I'm so darn thrilled. "You know me too well. Seriously though, do you think I look overdone for school?"

"I don't believe for a second that you would care. However, you are a little borderline for getting past Dad. You might want to slip out before he sees you. Then again, if you wait until the last minute to leave, I doubt that it is heavy enough for him to make you late by forcing you to wash it off."

God, it is so perfect, yet I can't help but want more. "Didn't Elizabeth Taylor have a beauty mark? What if we put one right—"

"You're done." The *thunk* of the eyeliner pencil Bailey drops into my makeup case drives home her point. "Don't mess with my masterpiece. Besides, I need to get out of here. I've got a new class starting today."

I can't stop looking in the mirror. I look fun, wild, and— Oh my God, I look freaking glamorous! I can't imagine people giving me a bad time like Bailey thinks they might. Then again, wearing neon green tights with a yellow skirt made them go crazy. What gives others the right to be judgmental over *my* wardrobe?

I just don't feel done though. This little splash of color is pretty, but it is too sedate for who I feel I am.

"Oh no you don't," Bailey warns.

"What? I haven't said or done a thing other than look in the mirror."

She wags a finger at me. "I know you. That beauty mark comment was the tip of the iceberg. We're on the verge of getting us both in trouble now. Give it a couple weeks before we push the envelope, okay?"

Reluctantly I agree. "It's a deal." I hate it when she is right.

I head out, on time, with an excited kiss of approval from Mom and a hesitant compliment from Dad; yet when I put my hand on the doorknob, I am reluctant to leave. There is something missing. Something key that I need to do …

Like a bolt, I race to the bathroom and pound on the door. When Bailey answers, I drag her out. "Come on, you need to drive me."

"What? You aren't late, and I have to go to—"

"GranGran needs to see this."

She tries to blow me off. "We can go after school."

"No. You won't be home until late. Let's go!" Still, she doesn't budge. Her face reeks of me being an annoying little sister. I give one last, grand plea. "Come on! She is going to be so proud of us. I really want her to see this while it is fresh. Remember how when you wanted to go to beauty school, she was the one who stood up for you? Don't you think she deserves to—"

Bailey throws her head back. "Fine! I'll meet you in the car."

Ten minutes later we are pulling into GranGran's driveway. I sprint up the walkway while on my cell phone with her. "Okay, open the door … now."

The door flies open like the woman is a teenager who is eager to see a friend. She drags me inside to get a good look. I chuckle at her yoga attire. I must have caught her on her way out. That's a huge relief. She has really had me worried.

She clasps her hands together. "Gorgeous! It is absolutely gorgeous! Tell Bailey I have the utmost faith in her abilities. Now, both of you go get to school on time and knock them dead!"

We are just out of the driveway and Bailey has hit the accelerator when GranGran dashes out as fast as needing a cane will let her. I roll down my window in haste, but we are already too far away. Mid way across the lawn, she stops and blows us a kiss.

"I am so proud of you. Never let anyone quell your spirit or silence your voice. I love you and Bailey with all my _"

That was the text GranGran was typing to me when she died. Based on what the paramedics found, I put together that when she got back inside she typed part of it, called them, then kept typing until God took her. That's how much she loved me.

She knew her body was failing. She should have sat down. She could have picked up a picture of her children and held it to her heart, but no, she chose to encourage the growth of my spirit.

For hours I have tried to take my eyes off of this message, but every time I look away a knife seems to jab its way into my heart. As long as I have this message, she can't really be gone, can she? Then again, maybe if I can just bring myself to focus on something else, I will wake from this nightmare.

A tuft of hair falls into my face. Rox tucks it behind my ear and forces a smile. When I got the news at lunch, she and Jacqueline raced me home. It is nearly midnight and we've been sitting on my bed and crying ever since. "GranGran was a true wonder," Rox says. "Remember when she taught me how dresses are structured so I could alter my thrift store finds? Until then, my wardrobe looked like I dragged it out of a bin for homeless people. Outcasts like us would be lost without free-spirits like her."

Rox looks so different with all of her crazy eyeliner cried off—like a little girl lost. It could not be more obvious that her love of hippie and mod fashions is seeded deep in her soul. Her passion for what she calls The Golden Age of Music runs so deep that her father gave her the nickname of Rox, a homonym for rock and roll. The name could not be more perfect.

Seeing Rox looking so out of her element drives home that GranGran was right. I do need to be true to myself—like really true. I won't live a lie any longer. I won't let GranGran down, and I certainly will not go to her funeral looking like someone other than who I know I really am.

I pop up from my bed like a shot from a cannon. If Bailey won't help me, or if anyone protests, I'll go to a salon first thing tomorrow and let a stranger do it.

Bailey sits in her room, staring at the wall. I turn

GranGran's phone to face her. The message shows loud and clear, even through our tears. "You got any bleach?" I ask. "I'm not letting anyone stop me."

Bailey nods and heads for her supplies.

I promise you, GranGran, no one will ever quell my spirit. In fact, it is time for it to soar.

Christmas Wrapping

The Present

No matter what paths I choose to take, destiny dictates that on Friday nights there are no forks in the road, only the way to Mulligan's. I'd like to say the events that originally led my friends and I here, all those years ago, were pretty normal but … Well, nothing in my life has ever been what most consider normal.

The day we first walked through that dive bar door had already been epic. Rox and I work for Endeara Candies, the company that makes the inedible stuff you find in the dark recesses of drug stores. Since I spend my time in the reception area, right between the elevator to the offices and the door to manufacturing, I often find myself smack in the middle of ridiculous situations.

On that day that led us here, the head of sales was sweating bullets while awaiting targets for what would be the sales pitch of the decade. Suddenly, shrieks came from the warehouse. The door flew open, and the crew emerged, covered in glops of red. Our hearts darn near stopped, but our panic slipped into confusion when the crew started laughing. A jellybean tumbler had malfunctioned, and engrossing syrup made everyone in splashing distance look like Slasher film victims. Not only was the goo tracked all over my lobby, but also when one of the workers slipped, his smacking butt splattered the liquid onto the pants of the head of sales. The guy flipped out—screaming like a banshee while doing zip to rectify the situation.

Just outside the door, people in designer suits were getting out of cars that might as well have had gold-plated dollar signs for hood ornaments. I paged the janitor, but also took no chances. After two decades of friendship, all it took to get Rox dashing to my aid was a call with me whimpering, "Red dye. Help, please."

The sales guy managed to stall the guests while Rox and I used every napkin and towel we could get our hands on to clean the mess. In true Endeara style, the janitor had gone missing. Rox and I got roped into helping in the warehouse as well. When all was said and done, we were so covered in crusting sugar that we looked like rejects from the Peeps factory.

Jacqueline's day had not been much better. She's a marketing person for Sporting News Today. She also has features that would make a director crazy not to cast her as Wonder Woman. Sometimes a single glance from Jacqueline can put a guy on the verge of selling his soul for a chance to be with her. However, all that beauty also results in none of the men at work taking her seriously. That day she had dealt with more than her fair share of sexist idiots.

We were barely able to function enough to pick a restaurant, let alone order food. Afterwards, going to bed sounded like riding a cloud to Heaven, but the need to blow off steam seemed just as great. However, the last thing any of us wanted was to go to a club filled with bad music and men with cheesy pick up lines. Once we had finished gorging on Chinese food and the fortune cookies had arrived, we didn't have long to come up with an alternative to watching bad movies and pigging out on ice cream.

Jacqueline groaned when I handed her a cookie. "Great," she said, "with the day I've had, this will likely be one more thing telling me something I already know, like 'Confucius say: Men can't deal with women in their domain.' Seriously, my determination to break down barriers seems futile."

All through dinner, Rox had barely been able to keep her eyes open. But somewhere between taking her last bite of rice and us getting the check, her glow of life came back. She had become so perky that just handing me my cookie made her DayGlo bangle bracelets clank a tune all their own. "We are no longer griping," she said. "I have absolute faith that our luck is about to flip on its head."

Her new-found enthusiasm breathed life into me. I ripped open the wrapper, cracked the cookie, and yanked out the fortune. " 'All you need is right in front of you.' " Okay, so it wasn't exciting, but it was right. The world could come crashing down, but as long as I had my friends, all was good.

I toyed with my cookie's wrapper while Rox ripped into hers. Despite the return of my ambition, fatigue was causing my vision to blur. Somehow though, the print was as obvious as my multi-colored mane—*Daisy Fortune Cookie Company, San Francisco, California.*

Oh wow.

The significance hit deeper when Rox read her fortune, " 'A fantastic adventure waits.' "

"I think you should have gotten that yesterday," Jacqueline said.

"Nope!" Rox stated with a bounce. "I told you, our world is about to change."

Boy was it ever, and someone was making sure I knew it.

Suddenly Rox's eyes went wide, and she gasped.

"Oh no," Jacqueline said with a tone of warning. "I know that look."

So did I. Rox was onto something. Although seeing the name of that cookie company had curiosity racing through my veins, I felt the urge to play along with Jacqueline. After all, it's just what we do. "Yeah, this is either going to be totally brilliant, or by the end of the night we will be praying for a cliff to drive over."

My money was on brilliant.

Rox pointed to my fortune. "Read this again, and then tell me what you see in front of you."

Jacqueline was fast to keep up the harassment. "A wack job in DayGlo who makes us need drinks."

"Exactly!" Rox thumbed to the window behind her. The

clank of her bracelets reinforced her command for attention. "Look behind me. Where have we always said we would check out and never have?" All eyes landed on the bar across the street—the same bar we sit in now.

That was years ago. In many ways, I feel like my butt has never left this stool. Back then, Mulligan's hadn't changed much since it opened in the fifties. Recently, the place was revamped to have a Victorian feel. The ornate, wood bar is stellar, but the stained glass windows are plastic. On the surface, Mulligan's is cool, but once you start paying attention to the details, you find that some things are not quite right. Regardless, here we are again.

Jacqueline raises her glass for a toast. "What shall we drink to?"

Rox adds her glass to the mix. Her board-straight, brown locks sway to their own beat. "To peace, love, and happiness," she says. Her toast is the perfect complement to her dress that is covered in yellow, white, and hot pink flowers. It would have had Twiggy crying with jealousy. People tell me I'm ballsy with my use of color. (Seriously, what is wrong with wearing bright, yellow shoes with an electric blue dress? As long as the saturation is right, it's ascetically all good.) However, when it comes to style, Rox's love of vintage fashion makes me look like a wallflower.

After a clank of our glasses we raise them to our lips, only to stop as if cued. Our eyes shift at each other in suspicion. Mulligan's has been refining its menu. We've opted to try the new specialty—Mexican Chocolate Martinis made with vanilla vodka, chocolate liquor, Irish Cream, and cinnamon. They sound great, but this is Mulligan's. In this place, you never know what you are in for.

Jacqueline shrugs, and we all dare to go in for a sip. The cold tribute to gods of old is filled with rich, chocolaty goodness that glides down my throat with ease. I pop up my head and scan the room. "Did we enter an alternate universe? This drink rules!"

Jacqueline sets down her glass with lightning speed and

drops her hands into her lap. "This is a bad sign. If the drinks are good, the clientele will change. If the clientele changes, Mulligan's will become trendy, and then we will never get a table. Worse, trendy places eventually crash and burn. We need to start scouting for a new hangout."

I smack my hand on the table. It's a little loud, even for me. Maybe it's the wine we had with dinner talking, but I can't help but blurt out my idea. "We should open our own bar! We can serve killer drinks, and we will make it part of the business plan to update the décor every few years so that we stay edgy. Finally, we can get out of our crappy jobs!"

Jacqueline groans, but Rox's eyes come alive. "That's a great idea! You know how crazy Martinis are all the rage while classic drinks never go out of style? One side of the menu will be all hip with new stuff and the back can be all retro with classics."

"Hip?" Jacqueline asks. "You are using the word hip to describe something modern? I already see a flaw, Granny."

"Hey! I may have a throwback vocabulary, but that doesn't mean my ideas are bad."

Jacqueline nods in agreement. "It is kind of interesting."

We may be onto something. Then again, we come up with new career ideas all the time. Once we start thinking them through, we find them to be crazy. However, I'm convinced that eventually one of us will come up with the right one. Right now though, I need another sip of chocolate perfection. Seriously, this stuff is …

Oh, wow.

Just above the rim of my glass, I catch a pair of eyes staring at me—electric-blue eyes attached to Heaven on legs. He's not all that tall. Maybe like five foot ten. He's got a slight tan, but then again, so does everyone here in Los Angeles. His medium-brown hair is combed over and fluffy on the top yet cleanly slicked on the sides—sort of like a James Dean-type, only without the overuse of hair gel.

He's also got that look—the one you expect to see accompanied by a wild amount of tattoos and a motorcycle helmet—yet judging by his pushed-up sleeves, all he has are the leather jacket, tattered jeans, and boots. The man who stands next to him is a more extreme version—tall, bulky, inked to the gills—the full biker persona. They look to be polar opposites, yet something about them screams peas in a pod. I'm intrigued.

Rox catches my peering and looks at the guy. "Wow! He's cute!"

Cute, hot, in desperate need of my affection—he's all of those. I can't stand the in-your-face look, so his subtlety has me pining.

We start playing the glance/get caught/turn game. It's lame, like two mice playing cat and mouse. I hate games, but sometimes you need to play them while you figure out what to do, just like now. I'm not so sure I'm willing to buy. This guy has a look in his eyes that says he knows he is good looking; however, when I catch him staring, how he turns away implies modesty. Modesty revs my engines.

Words are exchanged when his friend catches on to our game. His friend nudges his head in my direction like he is coaxing the guy to talk to me. Personally, I think that is a wonderful idea.

After another swig of his beer, my dreamboat stands. Rox nudges me. "Look! Mr. Super Cute Hottie is on his way."

Jacqueline peers in his direction. "Wow! He is gorgeous. Let's hope he doesn't know it."

"Oh, he knows it!" Rox says. "How could he not?"

Mid way to me, he sidesteps toward the bathroom. It is just as well. I'm not really crazy about forward men. Then again, how do you meet someone if you don't say hello?

He pauses, and then heads towards me again. The closer he gets, the more his back straightens, his head raises, and his jaw squares. The air of modesty he had while sitting with his friend disappears along with the tingle of my hormones. I love confidence, but I have too much self-respect to waste my time kissing up to someone with attitude. If a man wants to leave me begging for more, he doesn't hang up without saying goodbye; he tells me he can't wait to see me again.

James Dean II is just a couple of feet away when he suddenly looks like he wants to scamper home. My hormones come rushing back, and "hello" blurts out of me before he can change his mind.

His voice is soft and on the verge of cracking as he returns the greeting. Rox and I shift in our stools so he can stand between us. "Hi. I'm Chris," he says to me.

Wow! No cheesy pick up line? This is great. "Hi, I'm Darla."

He then introduces himself to the girls before turning back to me. We smile at each other like idiots.

He came to me, so he should open the conversation, right? But I said hello first. Then again, I hate games, and who speaks first really doesn't matter a hill of beans in the grand scheme of things. The better question is, who put the Mexican Jumping Beans in my stomach?

Finally, he breaks the ice. "I'm sorry, I should have thought of something to say. I hate pick up lines. I don't have a single decent one." He scratches his head while looking somewhat pained by the struggle for words. It's awesome. "You come here often?"

Jacqueline raises her glass. "Every Friday night for the last few years, no matter how hard we have tried not to."

Rox taps his arm. "Ask Darla if she wants to share an orange."

I groan. Jacqueline rolls her eyes. Chris's brows scrunch. "What?" he asks. "That's horrible. Somebody has actually used that on you before?"

Is that a slip of an accent in his voice? Southern?

Drool!

Jacqueline raises her hand. "Yep. You'd be amazed by the things we've heard."

"Wow," he says with raised brows.

Jacqueline and Rox turn to each other. Rox winks and Jacqueline nods. That genuine look of surprise just earned Chris their seals of approval. It must be obvious that I am interested, because they scoot over a stool and invite him to join us.

Chris removes his jacket before sitting. His short-sleeved T-shirt confirms that unlike his tatted friend, the only thing decorating his arms is a watch. Interesting. Clearly he does not mind tattoos on others, which is a good thing since my skin has not been pristine in years.

"I have to tell you," he says, "you are the most intriguing women I've ever seen." He looks to Jacqueline, who wears a fully buttoned blouse and a knee-length skirt. "I love your classic sense of style." Then he turns to Rox in her Go-Go dress and mod eyeliner. "Please tell me you dress like that all the time, because it absolutely suits you." Rox beams so much that I think I hear her squealing inside. Chris then looks to me yet can't quite make eye contact. "Your hair is stunning. The vibrant colors remind me of a peacock in its full glory." Finally his eyes meet mine. His mouth drops open to speak but then closes.

Are his cheeks flushing?

My heart flutters so much that I can't even pull myself together enough to thank him for the compliment.

Jacqueline comes to our rescue. "You have an interesting accent," she says to Chris. "Where are you from?"

"Alabama. Is it obvious? I'm really trying to lose it and fit in around here."

Jacqueline chuckles. "Trust me. Fitting in is overrated, especially in Los Angeles."

Rox is quick to agree. "I've never had any idea how it feels to fit in."

I'm with them. "The last time I tried was in grade school, just before I met you two. I am never making that mistake again!"

Chris looks at each of us in disbelief. "Wow, you have all known each other that long? That's some friendship."

The guy Chris was talking to earlier approaches our table. My eyes lock on his ink that covers the skin on the back of his hand and continues all the way up his arms. More color peeks out from under his T-shirt collar and climbs up his neck, stopping just shy of what would be his hairline. His art is a great big contrast to itself. The tattoo coming up the back of his neck appears to be part of a large piece done by a true artist. However, his arms are a different story. Those tattoos are much smaller and appear to be spattered about like whims or possibly tales of adventure and survival. I'm betting this man has a lot of great stories.

Jacqueline scoots her stool over so he can join us. He puts a hand up, smiles, and shakes his head. "No, thank you. Hey, Chris, come on, man, we've got to go. The guys are here." My racing hormones stop and frown.

"Sorry," Chris says to me.

We stare at each other, both trying to conceal how awkward we feel. Out of the corner of my eye, I catch Rox buying me time by popping up from her seat to check out some of the color creeping out from under the guy's sleeve. "Hey! Is that an Aerosmith logo?"

His eyes brighten. "Yeah, sort of. It's a hybrid between that and Skynyrd. Chris came up with it."

"Wow! How is that even possible?"

So Chris is a tattoo artist without obvious tattoos? The mystery around him grows. "Hey," he says, "I know this is short notice, but with next weekend being Thanksgiving, tomorrow is the only Saturday night I have free for the next few weeks. Are you available?"

Volumes have been written on the subject of dating. I'm pretty sure every authoritarian would tell me to stick with the cat and mouse game, but I really hate nonsense. "What did you have in mind?"

A group of biker-types calls for the attention of Chris and his friend. "How about I meet you here at six and we go from there?"

"Sounds great."

His eyes seem to twinkle. You'd think with all these other guys around he'd try to hide it. "It's a date," he says.

Maybe it is the excitement of the upcoming holidays that

provides the magic I feel seeping through the air, but it sure would be nice to have it caused by something else. The holidays have always held joy for me in so many ways. Dare I hope this one will bring magic of a different kind?

Thunder storms from outside, announcing that wheels are about to roll. My adrenaline rushes at the sound.

Jacqueline fans herself. Her eyes beam with sparks of mischief. "He is so not your type. I think you'd better leave him in my hands."

"He is so cute and perfect for you!" Rox adds.

I raise my glass in a silent toast to myself, but I don't keep all of my thoughts secret. "Yeah, isn't it awesome!"

Santa Claus Wants Some Lovin'

I feel lame.

A grown, reasonably attractive woman, sitting in a bar, waiting, alone, on a Saturday night—it just shouldn't happen.

Driven by both frustration and boredom, I send Bailey a text. *"He's late."*

Why did I put myself in a spin to get here on time? Aren't women the ones who are supposed to make men wait? Maybe I should have done that.

No, I hate being late just as much as I hate dating games. I also believe in making a good first impression.

My phone chimes with a return message from Bailey, *"And yet men always complain about us."*

Shoot, even if I was late, I might have been sitting here alone. It is nearly ten after six. He did say six tonight, didn't he?

"How long is it polite to wait for someone you don't know?" I text back. *"At what point do you become a chump?"*

Finally, I am hit with a wave of relief that I no longer need to badger myself with questions. Chris heads straight to the table were we met last night, even though it is dirty, and looks for a waitress to clear it. It would probably seem odd to most that he didn't just grab another table, but to me, it's sweet. My dad is sentimental like that. If I could score someone who is half the man he is, I'd be set.

My phone chimes with another text from Bailey. *"I think you know how to take care of yourself better than anyone else ever could."*

"He's here," I reply before tossing the phone into my purse.

I clear my throat, twice, and chuckle before it catches his attention. Chris smiles to the waitress, thanks her anyway, and heads to my booth. His walk reminds me of that of his friend last night—board-straight, confident, and with a bit of swagger. I can't help but notice that his hair is unkempt like he just got out of bed.

"Hey," he says. He sits across from me and places his cell phone on the table, taking care to make sure it is straight and aligned with the wood grain. I then notice that for as casual as he looks, everything about him is pristine. His ripped jeans seem pressed, his T-shirt is bright white and practically fresh out of the wrapper, and his boots and leather jacket have been polished. A woody scent, accented with a hint of mint and lemon, wafts across the table. It makes me want to snuggle into his shoulder. When I die, this is how I expect Heaven to smell.

Chris raises his hand to get the attention of the waitress. The smile he gives her would make the Devil envious of its power. She blushes to the point where she has to force herself to look at me and ask for my order. I don't blame her. He really is handsome, and that disheveled, yet perfectly clean, look could rev any woman's engines.

I don't want to drink anything too strong, so—

"A Cosmo for the lady. Whisky for me. Neat."

The waitress tucks her hair behind her ear as she turns to Chris. "Anything else?"

Did he just order me a *Sex and the City* drink without asking? I want to be polite, but I really dislike Cosmos.

I stop the waitress before she leaves. "Make mine an Old Fashion, please." Chris's expression goes blank. He is probably nervous and was trying to be nice by ordering for me. I stomped on it by ordering something that an eighty-year-old man would get. His unintentionally being rude doesn't justify me doing it to him. "Sorry, I'm not very fond of cranberries." I'm not exactly crazy about Old Fashions either, but I couldn't think of anything else. I must be just as nervous.

Chris leans onto the table and speaks softly. "So, you are a multi-faceted woman who does not want to be around cranberries. Tell me what else I get to learn about you."

Dear God, those eyes—so clear, so blue, so enrapturing.

Aw. I like the sweet way he said that. Yeah, we are both just nervous. It's understandable. "My job title says that I am Head of Reception Relations for Endeara Candies. What that really means is that instead of wearing professional office attire, I should dress like a traffic cop. I'm the first one who gets called in a crisis, be it an accident in the warehouse or one of the executives losing a paperclip."

His tone of voice strengthens. "Professional attire? With that hair?" He scoffs.

It has got to be nerves. Nerves will doom you. They are sure doing a number on me. I tuck my hands into my lap, suddenly very aware that they exist. "Yeah," I tell him, "I really don't get the place I work at. No one does. We all have to wear business suits and warehouse uniforms, yet individuality is stressed."

"Sounds interesting," he says, blandly.

Funny, how he is eyeing the room tells me nothing around here seems interesting to him. Maybe I am rambling. Lord knows my thoughts are. I don't quite feel like I am really here. "Yeah, there are always plenty of ridiculous antics going on. Rox works there too, so she helps keep me sane."

The waitress walks by on her way to take an order at another table. Chris flags her down with a single finger. It is pretty impressive that she noticed the stealth gesture. Then again, he is hard not to notice. "Hey, didn't we order drinks?"

"I'm sorry," she replies. "There was a mistake. The bartender is finishing them now."

She is hardly out of earshot when he says, "Looks like her daddy was the one who made a mistake."

My hand smacks onto the table. "What!" No! No possible way! That comment brought me back to reality with lightning speed. "What did you just say?" He's got two seconds to tell me I have wax in my ears and heard him wrong. Nerves or not, there is never an excuse to look down on someone like that.

Suddenly, he chuckles. While it may sound nervous, a layer

of smug coats him as if someone smacked his face with a brush. I'd kind of like to do that myself.

I'm pretty sure it is my obvious lack of amusement that gets him to stop laughing and change his tone. "I'm sorry. I'm not very good at this dating thing. With the way she was flirting with me earlier, I just wanted to make sure you knew there was nothing to be jealous over."

Um … Wow.

"Anyway … " He taps on the table and eyes the room. He is probably trying to figure out how to pull himself out of his hole. "So, that cute, little friend you work with, I bet she'd drool over what I have in the garage."

This guy makes zero sense. "So, you don't want me to be jealous over the waitress smiling at you, yet you are talking about making my best friend drool?"

His chin raises, and I swear he is puffing out his chest. "All right. Tell me what you drool over."

Okay, where is the hidden camera? I'm alternating between being pissed off and feeling like he is trying to make me jealous of pretty much every woman in existence. But what really gets me is my own behavior. Normally I don't just let others ask the questions; I interact. I don't sit with my hands in my lap; I gesture. I toss them in the air. I use them like a natural part of my vocabulary. I've always been that way. I don't like me like this, and no guy is worth me not liking myself.

The waitress returns with my Old Fashion. What I ordered must not have registered with her before, because she looks confused by the old man drink. I smile and thank her. She then places Chris's drink in front of him, and he fails to bat an eye. As she heads off, I thank her on his behalf. My confusion over his difference in behavior must show. "Something wrong?" he asks.

"Nope. Everything is hunky dory." Great, now I am telling lies. I never lie unless it is absolutely necessary. Can this man make me any more uncomfortable with myself?

Now I get a charming smile. "Excellent." He *clanks* his

glass to mine even though I've yet to touch it. His eyes hone in on me. "Drink up," he says, firmly.

God, those eyes. They have the power to suck me in like a fool. However, my sense of self-worth doesn't give a crap about my hormones. That voice was commanding. Come to think of it, most of our conversation has consisted of him giving passive orders. Something is not quite right here. I have to admit that I am morbidly curious as to what the hell is going on.

His phone rings. He doesn't even look at it before saying, "Excuse me," and heading off.

Maybe it is egotistical, but I have to question what could be so important that he would leave a first date for a phone call. Isn't this when we are supposed to put our best foot forward?

Yes, it is, which makes that supposedly well-intended joke about the waitress all the more crass.

Chris makes his way back to the table while still on the phone. "Sure, meet me there at six tomorrow. It's a date."

A date at six tomorrow? Am I over reacting by thinking that sounds familiar? Then again, with the way he seems to be trying to make me jealous, him making a date in front of me is fitting.

"So," he states while slipping his phone into his back pocket, "I know this was a short notice thing, but you're free after this, right? Finish up." He knocks back his whisky with one swallow. His glass hits the table, and I get dead on eye contact. "Let's get out of here." He then nudges toward my glass to drive home his point that it is time to go.

Seriously, what the hell? That's it. I'm done.

It's sad that I waited this long to call it quits, but I keep hoping to see the man I saw yesterday. Whoever he was, I liked him. He warmed my spirit. He made me want to know more about him. And he didn't make me feel like I am expected to follow his every command like a well-trained circus animal. This guy wants to suck me in by playing on my natural, female instinct to change him into what I saw he could be. He thinks it would buy him forgiveness every time that he is an ass. Little does he know I've never been one of those women who felt that trying to change anyone was either morally right or worth the time and dignity I would lose while failing.

It is long past time to go. "Actually, I need to call it a night. Busy day tomorrow." I slip on my jacket before reaching into my purse to foot my share of the bill.

There goes that blank stare again. It caves way to wide eyes when he realizes that I am serious about leaving. He places a hand out to stop me from paying. "I've got this."

I put down my share anyway. I won't let this guy find any reason why I could possibly owe him anything. "Thank you, but I have a personal policy about these things. Goodbye."

I'm nearly to the door when I hear boots running up behind me. "It's dark out. Let me walk you to your car."

Normally I would see this as a nice gesture, but right now the offer comes off as yet another passive form of assertiveness. My stride does not falter. "I'm fine. Thank you." Still, he follows along.

"I'll call you," he says as I get into my car, and then he just stands there.

It feels like he wants me to ask when or to throw open my arms and beg him to come to my place. I feel so cold for leaving like this, but I just want out of here. "Okay, good night."

I've got one foot in my car when his words race out. "I'm headed out of town on Monday for Thanksgiving. I won't be back until Sunday. I'll call you then, okay?"

I stop myself just short of saying I won't answer, because I won't lower myself and be rude. Also, it hasn't dawned on him that he doesn't have my number, and there is certainly no need to go there.

I can't drive off fast enough. It pains me to admit that books on dating may have a purpose other than being kindling after all.

I grumble about it for a bit on the phone with Bailey

before winding up at a movie with Rox. By the time I get to my apartment I've pretty much forgotten about the entire incident; that is, until I step into my bedroom. The daisy hair clips that GranGran gave me for my sixteenth birthday trail across the floor, forming a path from her picture to the closet where I keep the Ouija board. She has only done this one time before—over a decade ago when she taught me how to contact her.

March 13, 2001

"I hate school! I absolutely can't stand it!"

Actually, school is not the problem; it's my simple-minded classmates who waste all of their brain activity by trying to look like the latest pop star. Individuality is something they can't imagine, let alone spell.

Why do people feel the need to bully others for being different? GranGran always said that some people are afraid to be themselves, so they make fun of those who have less fear. If this is the case, my high school is brimming with scaredy cats.

The screen door *smacks* behind me. It's not loud enough for how angry I feel, so I slam the front door with all my might. I want the walls to be as rattled as I am. People are such jerks!

My backpack gets plopped onto my desk, and I fall back onto the bed to stare at the ceiling. Nothing in this world makes sense. Like, why is it we decorate walls but not ceilings? Is it because we like the idea of open air above us? That we equate white hovering over our heads with Heaven? Isn't Heaven supposed to be beautiful? I'd rather see some beauty than a white wall that is so over glorified that it gets its own name.

I roll to look at my wall that is purple—a power color. That's what I need right now, to keep feeling strength. The pink wall on the other side of me is too soothing.

But the colors seem faded compared to GranGran's photo that sits on my nightstand. What I wouldn't give for her to be here now.

I pull the picture toward me, and something falls to the floor. Over the edge of the bed I catch sight of one of the daisy hair clips she gave me for my sixteenth birthday. What is that doing out? I haven't worn one of those since her funeral two months ago.

I go to swipe it up when another one, sitting a few feet away, catches my eye. Then I see another one, and then another. Those are kept tucked away in a drawer. Was someone snooping in my room?

A rush of panic hits. No one should touch those clips but me. If I am missing a single one, I'll be sick for the rest of my life.

A fifth clips sticks out from under my closet door, which someone left open. This makes no sense. Bailey always asks before borrowing things, and everyone knows anything from GranGran means the world to me and thus must be treated with care.

I get down on my hands and knees in search of the last clip. I look behind boxes, inside my shoes, and then under them. Nothing. My heart starts pounding over the thought of losing my sixth, beloved clip.

I toss my hands up. "What the hell is going on?"

A gleam of light, coming from above, catches my eye and makes my breath halt. I have to be dreaming. Why is a clip attached to the Ouija board GranGran gave me?

I try to shake off the notion of something mysterious happening. Bailey must be messing with me.

But why would she leave my clips—

In a trail …

I've been following a trail of daisies—a trail connecting the final gifts GranGran gave me.

A new kind of excitement races through me. I know GranGran believed in this stuff, and I guess I always have too, but that doesn't change the fact that it seems unreal. I've been visited!

Or am I *being* visited?

My eyes scan the room for an image, another sign, anything that would show that I am not alone, yet all is quiet.

These clips are a signal. While the reason for giving me the Ouija board became apparent when she died, I've barely allowed the thought of using it to enter my mind. What if it didn't work? It would be heartbreaking to know that GranGran had such faith we could talk again, only to have it shatter.

Or would that really be the case? A Ouija board is just a toy, right? If I can't reach her, it could be because she is busy doing something else.

I start to go for the board, but fear gets the best of me. I so want all of the mystical things she believed in to be true. I want to know that there is more than the here and now. Most of all, I want to believe GranGran is still out there.

My actions happen without another thought—the curtains are yanked closed, a candle is lit, and I sit on the floor with GranGran's picture next to me. I'm a ball of fire, determined to make this work. Without a doubt, this is what she intended when she said to follow the daisies.

I expect the new board to crackle when opened, but the sound that fills my ears seems to come from the wave of energy that pours out of it and washes over me. There is a reason why this was given to me without the plastic wrap still on it, and it isn't only because GranGran stuck a second gift inside the box. She had special friends, and I am betting that one of them did something to this board. That thought deepens my faith.

But my flame starts to quell as I pick up the other gift that sits in the box—the one that she told me to open when the time is right. Now I am certain she was referring to the time after her death. If I don't do this right, her last wish will falter. I start to place the gift back into the box. I couldn't bear the heartache of letting her down.

No, self-doubt means failure. I owe her more than that.

My fingers tear into the blue, metallic paper. I gasp at the sight of vibrant colors that quickly become obscured by tears. GranGran loved to paint. In her golden years her hand became unsteady, so picking up a brush was a rarity. I smear away the tears so that I can behold what is probably GranGran's last piece of art. She painted petals around the window of an antique, wood planchette, turning it into the center of a flower. The pain of missing her sinks into my gut, but my love for her makes my heart bloom. "Follow the daisies," I utter in awe.

My sniffle is hard and deep. I always knew she loved me, but it has never hit my soul as much as it has at this moment. The day I got this, Bailey got a savings bond because at some point she will need to be saved. GranGran gave me a board and a planchette painted with a flowering daisy so I could grow. Even though she is gone, she is still helping me bloom. "Thank you, GranGran, because even if this doesn't work, I am thrilled that you loved me enough to do this."

With a deep breath, I grab my focus and try to tune out the world. "Okay. Are you there?"

I wait, but all I hear are dogs barking in the distance. I also don't sense anything new.

I deepen my focus and try again. Although all I continue to hear are the dogs, the energy coming off the board grows. Is it working? Please God, let it be working.

I feel like the board is glowing, yet there are no visual signs to confirm that. However, the greater my determination, the more the electricity vibrates. My eyes snap to GranGran's photo as if she has called my name. My vision begins to blur as energy swirls around me. The dogs outside go so crazy that it is hard not to let them steal my focus. "Are you there, GranGran?" I whisper, fearing a normal tone will cause me to lose whatever ground I think I have gained. This has to be working. All of this must be amounting to—

The planchette jerks, gliding its way to "*Yes*". The hair on my arms raises. It's working!

I try to be patient and wait for more. I have so many questions about what I am going through, and so many questions about what has happened to her, yet right now I can't think of a single one. I just want to feel her near me again.

The intensity of the barking grows. Why won't those dogs shut up? They keep getting louder and—

Suddenly my hands skate across the board. *"F-O-C-U-S,"* I am told.

My heart recalls everything about her—her perfume, her laugh, all the happiness she brought into the world. The planchette rattles as if it is trying to jump off of the board. A breeze brushes my hair back like I have wings, yet the flame on the candle refuses to go out. Despite the natural urge that nearly pushes me out of the house while running in fear of the unknown, I hold my ground.

Suddenly, energy rips through the room, shaking the walls. Then the rattling halts, the breeze stops, and my hair drapes back down. All sounds fade into silence, until the voice of a young woman fills the air. "Do not take your hands off of that planchette."

Azure mist creeps across the board, and then whips up like a blaze. A shadowy image forms, reminding me of a genie coming out of a bottle. My heart races with glee at the woman with long auburn hair, green eyes, and a stunning figure that is shown off by a form-fitting mini-dress. In so many ways, she is a beauty to behold. If she had not warned me to keep my hands where they were, I would jump up to hug her. "GranGran!"

"Did you miss me?"

I laugh in relief. "You know I did!"

"Well, now you have me back. I *love* what you did to your hair!"

Santa Claus Is Back In Town

The Present

The annoyance of my date with Chris earlier tonight has almost been erased by concern. Why is GranGran trying to contact me? It has only been a few days since our last chat, and I am always the one to contact her. Finding those clips has me worried.

Is there any reason to be worried for a ghost? It's not like she can take ill, can she?

Azure haze rises off of the planchette and spirals its way across the room. My words sprint out before her image fully forms. "GranGran, is everything okay?"

She places out her hand to quell my worries. Her smile is warm, much like I would expect of someone who is empathetic. For the first time I see her for what she may really be, an angel or a messenger of God. "Give him a chance," she says.

My brows twist. Is she kidding? For the first time in over a decade she is the one who contacts me, and it is over that loser? "Are you serious?" My hands smack onto the floor. "You've been watching. Is nothing sacred?"

"A person in my state doesn't so much watch as she senses. It's a loophole that keeps me from invading your privacy. Right now, I sense that this young man has you perplexed, not to mention a tad miffed."

How weird is it that I find talking to a spirit to be totally normal, yet I think this situation with Chris is freaky? "What is the deal with him?"

"Not all free spirits were influenced by those as accepting

as I am."

I put down the planchette and throw my hands back like I am not just tossing in the towel but throwing it away. I'm long past the need to hold onto anything to keep my focus. I just treat GranGran as if she were as alive as ever. Her body is dead, not the important part. "Okay, not that I am complaining about you looking out for me, but why are you always willing to see things from so many angles? I thought mature people were supposed to be old fashioned and narrow-minded?"

GranGran balks and waves her hand at me. The gesture seems so old-lady like that it doesn't fit her young body in the least. Finally, she catches on to what I am really saying and drops her hands onto her hips in a huff. Yep, we are two peas in the same cartoon pod. "Are you calling me old?"

I make a show of tapping my finger to my chin. "Hmm … Remind me what year you were born." She gives me an *oh, please* look, and I laugh at the woman who currently appears to be my age. "I would never dare. Dead or alive, you are still the most liberal and lively person I know. Seriously, teenagers could learn from you."

GranGran plops herself down on the floor and sits criss-cross. She then bounces a bit while looking satisfied to be agile again. Even though she lost her arthritis-filled body long ago, she has never failed to appreciate regaining her mobility. "All past lives aside—"

I cut her off. "Wait, that reincarnation mumbo jumbo is real?"

She rolls her eyes like I should know better. She then actually bends in and gets in my face. Her tone reeks of wisdom and serves as another reminder that she is no spring chicken. "I was a product of the Jazz Age and was ninety-two when I died, meaning I was born in nineteen oh eight. Do you know what was happening when I was twenty? Prohibition. Not long before that started we were smack in the middle of World War I. While growing up, it seemed the father or brother of nearly every one I knew had died. After the horrors of war we needed to let loose, but thanks to Prohibition we couldn't have any fun. Then the Great Depression hit, and we couldn't afford simple luxuries, such as sugar. It was either bow down to misery or seek a bit of freedom. Freedom meant rebellion. Rebellion, or lack there of, is what shapes a person."

My mind locks onto visions of lonely widows and children without shoes, all seeing no escape from a life covered in dust. At least I can afford to grab my friends and head out to Mulligan's. Even if we had to forgo the cocktails, we still have shoes, and expensive ones at that. Knowing GranGran though, I can't help but ask, "Please tell me you made bathtub gin."

She winks.

I smack my hand on the floor. "Wow! Really?"

"Your Great Grandfather was resourceful in many ways, which is exactly why I married him." She snickers. "He says hi, by the way. Anyway, when I was in my twenties, I met a young woman who got sucked into what she thought was love, only to have him leave before she could tell him she was pregnant. Not only did her family reject her so badly that she had to move half-way across the country, but even strangers called her a tramp and treated her like dirt. She was a good person in a bad situation—so bad that she had to turn into the tramp everyone accused her of being just to survive. While everyone else was spitting on her, I took her in and gained a second family. That whole experience showed me that just because a person has challenges, it doesn't mean her heart is different from that of anyone else. If we could each open our eyes and see that not understanding a person does not make him less human, this world would be a better place."

This makes so much sense. Our experiences are not just the things we live through, but also what we see others endure. We can grow from the misfortune of those around us. "So that is why you always encouraged my free spiritedness."

"It is also why you grew up knowing that everyone is beautiful and deserves a chance, whether you understand *him* or not."

Yeah, I knew this is where we were headed. "Even someone who tries to cover the fact that he is egotistical and controlling?"

Now I get a finger pointed at me—another family trait. "Not at all. Normally I would tell you to go with your gut, and then if you tried to see him again, I would arrange for a lightning bolt to weld the lock on your apartment so you couldn't leave. However, this time I am asking you to give him one more shot."

If this were anyone else, I would ask if she were joking. Still, I have to question if we are talking about the same guy. "Really? The guy on a power trip? The guy with the cocky sense of humor that is more rude than amusing? I can't possibly understand why."

She reaches for my hands. What I wouldn't give for her to actually be able to grab them again. Nonetheless, her love seeps into me. "Because you had me in your life and Chris didn't. Think about what you would have been like if you were not supported. What rebellion would you have gone through to find yourself?"

"So you are telling me that—"

She raises a finger to stop me. "I am not telling you anything that you don't already know deep down inside. And I am not trying to interfere with your love life, just to ease your mind."

"Love life? Who said I had him pegged for a love interest?"

She tosses her head back with a laugh. "That fine piece of manhood with the streak of playful boyishness! Oh, please!"

Yeah, we both know the man is so hot my skin nearly melts off every time I think of him.

"Seriously though, that is for you to decide. I am only saying to relax a bit. Besides, I have never led you astray. Look at how I guided you to Mulligan's. Trust me, there are many reasons why you frequent that place."

Is she real? Man, I hope there is a good reason that we

choose to plant our butts in that crappy place week after week.

GranGran kicks her seriousness up a notch. "Honey, I know a woman must always proceed with caution. I am also very proud of you for not letting yourself get wrapped up in someone that wants you to compromise who you are. However, there is a difference between being careful and restraining your spirit. You need to trust me that this case is not what it appears." Her image and words trail off as she bails without giving me a chance to further grill her. "Allow yourself to see where this can lead. Kiss Bailey for me when she gets into town for Thanksgiving."

I hate how brief these visits are. Why can't she stay a little longer and bake cookies with me or sit down for tea like we used to do? She is right though. Chris may put a dancing bed of flowers in my gut, but my attraction to him isn't only brought on by lust. On the night we met, something about him spoke to my soul. I won't let myself be afraid to hear what he has to say. However, he has to come to me, and I won't tolerate the attitude I saw tonight. I may trust GranGran, but I also won't put up with anybody's bull.

Someday At Christmas

Mulligan's may not be the hottest place around, but this Friday night it is practically a ghost town. Then again, I'm still so full from last night's Thanksgiving dinner that it is a miracle the stool hasn't collapsed under me.

"Holy Mama Cass," Jacqueline says. "I ate so much last night that I am still full."

Bailey nearly loses the sip she just took by laughing it out of her nose. Rox's head snaps towards Jacqueline. Her narrow eyes say she wants to chew Jacqueline out over being mean to one of her idols, but her snicker shows that holding back a chuckle at the well-intended joke is hard. "Hey! Show some respect."

Jacqueline raises her glass. "To Ellen Naomi Cohen. Lord, I wish I had her talent. The best ones always die young."

In some ways that statement is true. The good ones never live long enough, no matter how old they get. I join Rox, Jacqueline, and Bailey in the toast to Mama Cass.

Rox turns to Jacqueline. "I'm surprised you know her real name."

Jacqueline puts her arm around one of her two, true best friends for life. There is no doubt that if one of us slipped into the gateway to Hell, the other two would dash in after her. "You have got to be the biggest rock and roll fangirl on the planet," Jacqueline says. "We met twenty-five years ago because our fathers were in a band together. We went through every grade of school together. We were roomies in college and we have been roomies for all of the seven years since. Do you really think I can escape knowing something as basic as Mama Cass's real name when you constantly rattle on about music? I do always listen to you." Jacqueline turns the partial embrace into a hug. "Always."

Rox snuggles into Jacqueline's shoulder. "Aw, you really do love me."

"Just like anyone would love her annoying little sister," Jacqueline tells her.

Bailey smirks. I give her arm a playful smack in return. She follows it up with a bear hug that crams my face into her shoulder, smashing my nose. Crammed face or not, I miss the hell out of her. Why couldn't she have gotten a killer job in Hollywood instead of all the way across the continent? The moon seems closer than she does. Regardless, I am so blessed; my sister is one of my best friends, and my best friends are like my sisters. How perfect is that?

Rox takes a sip out of her Milky Way Martini. Suddenly her eyes widen. I then become their target as they narrow. "You keep looking at the door."

"What? I do not!" Do I?

"Yeah, you do," Jacqueline adds.

"Face it," Bailey says, "you may be annoyed at that jerk, but you can't get him out of your mind. Something about the situation has your attention."

I come to my own defense. "That's ridiculous. Besides, he's not even in town now."

"All the more proof that Bailey is right," Jacqueline says. "It's okay. Feeling that way is fine, but acting on it is another story. He sounds like an ass."

My sigh isn't one of longing but more of frustration. GranGran gave me a lot of food for thought. It was so much easier when Chris was just a hot guy who turned out to be a jerk. Now I have no idea what to think. Then again, maybe I do. "The whole night was like watching a puppy who can't figure out what his paws are for, so he barks too much to cover his insecurity."

Jacqueline shrugs. "One day, the dating game has got to work out for one of us."

Rox's tilted head tells me I am being sized up. "Is that why you are thinking of giving him a second chance?"

How did she know? Once more, why does everyone else look unfazed?

"You are playing with your hair," Bailey says. "A woman twirls her hair around her finger when she is either flirting with a man or is thinking of the one she wants to flirt with."

I look to my finger and see some of my green locks wrapped around it. Crap! She's right.

Truthfully, everything about the whole situation makes me feel awkward. I hate people who come off as fake. All interference from GranGran aside, it is obvious that there is a genuine side to Chris that I find fascinating. Thing is, it should not be up to me to dig for it, just like no person should think he or she has the ability, let alone the right, to try to change someone. "You know how James Dean always seemed a little lost and rebellious against himself?" I ask. "Chris seems more rebellious about being lost."

There is that word again. What was it GranGran said about rebellion? How we rebel, or even if we choose not to, shapes us. She also asked what rebellion I would have gone through to find myself.

Rox nudges me and whispers, "Speaking of Mr. Rebel Without A Clue." She nods sideways, and I catch a glance of Chris. My heart goes into a sprint, and I reach for a napkin. Why are my hands suddenly clammy with excitement, yet I also feel the urge to flee? "Oh God. What is he doing here? He's supposed to be in Alabama."

Naturally, after I blurt that out, all heads snap in his direction.

"Oh, wow," Bailey says, sounding breathless. If she wants his drama, she can have it.

I start kicking the girls under the table so they will stop staring. They all jerk and make poor attempts at acting naturally. Jacqueline grabs her glass and looks to an empty booth. Bailey reaches into her purse for a mirror to check her eyeliner. Rox dips her head to take a sip from her straw, and then raises her eyes to me. Bailey and Jacqueline's eyes also snap in my direction. Nothing about any of this is covert. "I'm fine," I tell them. "I think."

Chris heads my way—at least, the guy looks like Chris, but he doesn't feel like the same person I attempted to have a conversation with. This man walks with hesitation, and his eyes have yet to make contact. The swagger of seduction is nowhere in sight. Neither is the air of smugness. In fact, everything about him says that he is a different person—a real person—not a poster child for arrogant misfits.

A few feet away, he brings his hand out from behind his back. Even though I can't make out the details through the paper wrapping, my pulse accelerates at the sight of a bouquet.

Is he here to try a different seduction tactic on someone else, or is he attempting to play a new game with me? Maybe, just maybe, this is the real him. GranGran would never ask me to give a second chance to someone who could truly cause me strife. Regardless, I hate that my heart is trying to sprint out of my chest at the sight of that jerk.

My grip on the napkin tightens as he closes the distance between us. Just like he did when we first met, he directs his hello to me before greeting the rest of the table. He is barely able to look at me when he asks, "Can I talk to you for moment?"

Part of me is still annoyed from his antics on Saturday night and wants to tell him I'm busy. However, the person I trust more than I will ever trust anyone, told me to give him another chance, and he does seem to know he blew it. I just hope this is not an act.

We take seats at the next table in such a way that he can sit without catching sight of the looky-loos known as my friends. Try as they might not to, they won't be able to keep from staring. I don't blame them. I would not either. It's just how we are.

"I owe you an apology," he says. "I was so wrapped up in being what I thought a woman wanted that I didn't respect the one in front of me. Here." As if he had not already thrown me for enough of a loop, my breath now shudders when I get a good look at the flowers. The bouquet of daisies has been dyed in a glorious rainbow of colors. "You are far from being a typical, rose girl. You are daisies. The vivid colors of your hair suit you not because they look good, but because you are a rainbow of beauty who isn't afraid to let the world see her shine. You are your own garden, much like how a bush of daisies is plentiful with life." He stops to twiddle his thumbs. "Look, I know that I was far from being the perfect date. I heard the frustration in your voice, and I don't blame you. Is there any way I can persuade you into a do-over?"

"A do-over?" The words barely come out of me. Daisies—how did he know? Is this GranGran's doing, or are these really coming from him? Maybe the flowers were his idea and she whispered the word daisies in his ear.

"Yeah," he says more to the table than to me, "I don't feel you're too keen on a second date. Maybe you would be willing to show a little mercy and grant me a do-over."

He's so sweet. So genuine. So the type of man I could appreciate. But is this the real him? Given his words, his mannerisms, the daisies, and what GranGran said, I can't help but feel hopeful. I also can't wipe the grin off of my face.

I play with a petal—a beautiful, hot pink petal that reminds me of my favorite lipstick—because as much as I try to fight the emotions that have blindsided me, my face feels flushed, and I don't know what else to do with my hands. "I think I can manage that. But why are you here? I thought you weren't coming back for a few days?"

He seems to put up a fight with himself to look at me. Seriously, what changed? I love this side of him.

Finally his voice wins the battle of his nerves. "Can I just say that it became pretty obvious that even if I had a way to reach you, you would not have answered when I called? I didn't make the best impression, but obviously you made a hefty one on me. Jacqueline said you always wind up here on Fridays. The longer I waited to do this, the more awkward it would be. Besides, if I'm to be totally honest, I had to do this quickly, else I'd let myself come up with excuses not to. I need to fix me." He rattles his head. "Sorry, that's a long story. I'll let you get back to your friends. I don't want to push, but can that do-over be tomorrow?"

He actually remembered what my friend said that first night, let alone her name? This is the man I was expecting that first date to be with. My heart feels so warm that I think it may be melting on to the floor. I have plans with Bailey for Saturday, but—

Bailey kicks behind her, catching the leg of my stool. My ears ring with her silent lecture that I would be insane to say no. "Yeah, I can make tomorrow work."

His smile does in the last bit of my heart that has not already turned to goo. "Can I have your number so I can call you in the morning and work out the details?"

Chris starts running his finger under the band of his watch like it has suddenly become tight. How he also sucks in his lower lip makes him seem concerned that I might say no or give him false information just to make him go away. It is so sweet that by the time I've finished writing my number, I'm genuinely okay with our situation. When he walks away, I even let myself feel hopeful.

Bailey steps up and puts her chin on my shoulder. Together we watch him go out the door. "You good?" she asks. The words may be hers, but I sense all of my friends asking as well.

"Yeah, I'm great."

We take our seats back with the girls. Bailey's gaze is locked on the flowers. She can't hide the mist forming in her eyes nor the crackle in her voice. "I heard what he said about the daisies. Sounds like something someone we love would have told you."

It does, and it is especially weird in light of what that special someone told me a few nights ago, but I don't tell Bailey that. It's not that she wouldn't believe me. I know she would. In fact, I wouldn't be surprised if she talks to GranGran as well. But GranGran gave me that board in private, so in private the resulting conversations will stay. It just seems right.

Rox reaches across the table and touches my arm at almost the exact time Jacqueline does. Their eyes are also locked on the flowers. "They are not just brightly colored because you are a rainbow," Rox says. "They are a neon sign trying to grab the attention of your soul."

Yes, and they worked. I hear you GranGran—loud and clear. But I won't give him the second chance you asked for. Chris has earned that do-over.

It's A Marshmallow World

My eyes scan down my body for yet another check. Something must be missing, because I feel off balance.

Okay, sweater? Check. Bra under said sweater? Check. Nice jeans? Check. Panties that there is no way he is seeing but are nice enough so that I won't be embarrassed if he rufies my drink? Check. Killer, over the knee boots with heels that can take out a man's junk, if necessary? Check. Coat to cover this awesome outfit? Check. Gloves to cover my jittering fingers because for some bizarre reason I can't freaking wait to see this guy again? Check. Sweating bullets because this coat is too heavy for California and my heart is racing? Double check.

From inside the living room, a woman on the TV asks, "What am I getting myself into?"

I yell to her, "I'm asking myself the same question."

Someone raps on the front door, and my eyes dart back to the mirror in panic.

This is lame! Being worked up over a guy who can be an ass one minute, and then be sweet as punch the next, is stupid beyond words.

I don't let myself think of anything more than turning off the TV, grabbing my purse, and answering the door.

I catch Chris scratching at his neck and undoing the top button of his pressed, grey, short-sleeved, button-down shirt. He's got on his signature, black leather jacket again, but this time his jeans are tear-free. He is also standing like a normal person—that is to say, he looks comfortable with himself—even though the situation seems to have him a tad on edge. I breathe relief in knowing I am not the only one.

Just like last night, not a speck of arrogance is in sight. However, what I do see now are two motorcycle helmets.

His smile has just the right touch of shyness. It's so comforting that it nearly causes the rufie-approved panties to fall. He hands me a helmet, only to then retract it. "Sorry, I didn't ask if you are okay with bikes. I mean, it seemed like you were the other day, but if you would rather drive—"

I laugh. "Wow. Do you really think I have never been on a bike before?"

His lips part, and he lets out a sigh that implies more relief than seems necessary. "I try to never take anything with a lady for granted. I thought you'd get a kick out of seeing that bike I mentioned."

Now I'm a little unsure about all this again. "You mean the one you think Rox would like?" I still can't see why he thinks my mod, Go-Go dress-wearing friend would dig a motorcycle. That is, until I walk outside and chuckle at his Vespa. A decked out, vintage, freaking Vespa in cherry condition! How many mirrors are on this thing?

He's right. Rox would love it. To her, the only thing that could surpass this as a white horse would be a classic muscle car that looks like it just rolled off the line. "Well, you did say bike and not motorcycle. This thing is awesome!"

"Really? You're not embarrassed? We could go get the Harley, but this seemed like it would amuse you more."

"Does it ever! My uncle taught me how to ride on a Harley. I've ridden so many that they mean zip to me, but I have never been on one of these."

"Wait, you know how to operate—"

"Are you kidding?" I stick my hand out. The bewildered man actually gives me the keys, and off we go.

"Ouch! Crap!" I say.

Chris laughs—again. My face reddens. I should have asked where we were going, but no. I let him direct me, turn after turn, until we were here—an outdoor ice rink whose perimeter is surrounded in fake snow and plastic pine trees that have been flocked with white goo. He can't believe that I haven't been ice-skating other than once when I was six, but I'm Los Angeles born and raised. In the winter, we would wear parkas as soon as the thermometer dropped below sixty, if they were not so unfashionable. No one here would know how to survive in actual snow, so all this synthetic stuff is fitting.

Chris kneels down and helps me up. He then tucks his arm around mine. I have to admit that it's pretty nice—safe-feeling even—which is still confusing. "You want to take a break?" he asks.

And leave this coziness? No way. "I'm fine, thanks. I refuse to surrender to the enemy."

"You see frozen water as an enemy?"

"Ice belongs in a cocktail shaker. By the way my feet are wobbling, they would be great at shaking Martinis."

"Note to self, Darla likes her drinks shaken, not stirred." He then turns to me. "If you are really James Bond in disguise, what does that say about me?"

"You own a vintage Vespa. Some would already say that you are comfortable with exploring your feminine side." My eyes are locked on the ice in fear of my next glide, yet the flow of banter shows my mind could not be more relaxed.

He shrugs. "At least you look more like a Bond girl than you do Sean Connery."

Hey, I've made it a few feet this time. Maybe I can manage this after all. I stop, straighten my back, and steady myself. I get one, two glides in and …

Bam! My butt becomes one with the ice.

Chris laughs. I try not to glare at him. "Sorry," he says while offering me a hand. "I have to admit though, I'm grateful for the um, icebreaker."

"Oh, cute, Chris. Real cute!"

Now he is really chuckling. So am I. "Sorry," he says.

I wait for it.

He laughs again.

Yeah, I thought so.

"No," he says while helping me to my feet, "I'm not sorry about that remark at all." All he gets out of me is an eye roll like I am annoyed, which he sees right through and laughs at. Then he turns serious. "You know how your feet are capable of getting you places, but inside those skates they need to find a new way to function? That's what is going on with me. I have had a heck of a time trying to figure out how to talk to you about it. It goes along with the explanation you are owed."

I must be looking like I think he is crazy. That comment is so much like my puppy dog remark about him that it is uncanny. He nudges his head toward some benches, wraps my arm in his, and glides me out of the rink. The seat is a welcome sanctuary.

"I'm not who you think I am," he says. "Actually, scratch that. I've no idea what you think, but whatever it is, I probably need to change it."

"You mean you are not some James Dean wannabe who is trying to convince people he is all that but knows he isn't?"

He blinks and his eyes go wide. "Wow. You are one amazing judge of character."

"Next you are going to tell me you are still a virgin."

He sucks in his lips.

No way!

Those big, blue eyes dart back to me and a smile cracks. "Okay, no, but truth be told, there has only been one woman. I wanted to marry her, but she kept putting it off. When I caught her in bed with some guy, I found out why. While my number of conquests remained at one, hers was nearing the triple digits."

Is he serious? Now I am beginning to wonder what is real again. From his expression and hint of a snicker, I'm pretty sure he is reading my mind about that right now.

"Do you believe in God?" he asks.

Yikes! The last time I was asked that was when a group of guys wearing pressed, white shirts and skinny black ties came to my door. Being asked that question before he even knows my last name makes me want to bail out of here.

Thing is, that little thing about Chris that keeps me interested isn't so little right now. I actually feel like I can talk to this guy, so I risk judgment and state what my heart tells me is right. "You know, the jury was out on that one for a long time. But events over the years have shown me that thinking we are superior beings who get their lights snuffed out upon death is arrogant on a huge number of levels."

"That's an interesting way of looking at it."

I shrug. "If we are so great, then how can we possibly be destroyed so easily? But if a part of us lives on, there is something more outside of life. Thus, we are not that great after all."

"Huh." Chris looks to the stars. There is depth to his voice that goes beyond physical tone. "That might be the only view on religion that hasn't scared the crap out of me."

"That's a relief. When you hit me with the God question, I thought I might be in for a sermon."

"Quite the opposite," he says, insistently. "Do you have any tattoos?"

What a weird non sequitur. To say this man has my curiosity up is an understatement. Where is this going? "Just one cluster of daisies."

"That's quite the coincidence. Can I ask why you got it?"

After all these years, the mention of GranGran still makes my heart sag. Still, I would not trade a second of the time we shared for anything. I have to wonder when, if ever, I will tell anyone the full meaning behind my affection for daisies and the woman who tells me to follow them. "They are a symbol of the most influential person that I will ever have in my life. I miss her, and the tattoo on my ankle is my way of showing her I am still listening, even though she is long gone."

"So, in a way, you can say that tattoo marks a testament to the beauty God brought into your life."

"Absolutely."

Chris pushes out a long sigh. Maybe it has more to do with

thinking about GranGran than anything else, but I feel like I am about to get whammied. "My devout, Southern Baptist family sees any markings or piercings as a sin that is certain to doom you to an eternity of fire and brimstone. Heaven forbid you pierce your ears and wear cross earrings. The thought of defiling your body and then showing any respect for the Lord makes you a Satanist in their eyes. In case you haven't figured it out yet, I've led a sheltered life that I have been trying to rebel against for years. Not only is my family unforgiving and judgmental, they are hypocritical. If Mom really felt defiling her body was a sin, she wouldn't weight three hundred pounds and pull dinner out of the deep fryer every night. I may be a firm believer, but my family's hypocrisy makes it hard for me to define what those beliefs are."

"Wow," is all that I can think to say. Chris's mystery may be unraveling, yet it gets more fascinating by the second. There are so many pieces to this puzzle—pieces that maybe even he hasn't been able to find.

Chris pulls out his iPhone and shows me a picture of a guy with a strong family resemblance. The guy could be his twin, except his hair is combed tight to his head. Also, the glasses and suit he is wearing make him look kinda dorky. Surrounding him are women in skirts and sensible shoes, along with men whose bland appearance make them look like they have been forged from the same mold. "Thanksgiving dinner with my family," he tells me. "That guy with the glasses is the me they know."

He can't be serious. He seems so different yet …

Yet so did he on our last date.

And now it all makes sense. No wonder why GranGran made a point of contacting me. Chris needs her kind of understanding. His only way to find it may be through someone who gets what it is like to be different. Someone who had guidance and encouragement when it was needed. Someone like me.

Suddenly I have so many questions. Each of them is more personal than I should ask someone I hardly know. Still, he is opening up to me, so I narrow it down to one question that covers the depths of my curiosity. "Chris, who are you really?"

He doesn't look offended by my nosiness. In fact, his features soften like I have become a long-needed friend. "I'm still figuring that out. I can tell you that I am a guy who loves noisy music that my parents call the work of the Devil. I love bikes—all kinds of them. And old cars that drive like boats. Piercings and tattoos are cool, yet I can't bring myself to get one for the fear of God that was put in me. Yeah, I wasn't exactly struck down when I lost my virginity before marriage, but I was serious about my intentions of being with only one woman."

Chris stares off. He seems to be talking to whatever lies within, searching for answers. "She wanted what she had been told was taboo. I just wanted to be me. The night I screwed up my date with you, I finally saw those are two different things."

It's hard to even begin to know what to say, but he is starting to make a lot more sense now. "I guess this explains why the man who wields a tattoo gun for a living doesn't have any himself." He turns to me with knotted brows of confusion. "Your friend said you created his tattoo."

He seems to search his brain until it hones in on something. His head drops, and he chuckles. "I'm not a tattoo artist; I am a graphic artist. I only designed that for him." He puts his hand out in a stopping motion. "I know I've said and implied a lot of things that make me sound like someone other than I am. In the interest of full disclosure, I'll tell you now. Carole and I met in jail because an animal rights demonstration went awry."

The mysteries of Chris just keep springing up. I'm so glad he asked me for another chance to get to know him. "Carole? The walking refrigerator's name is Carole?"

"Yes, Carole Kelly, and if you make fun of his name, humanitarian or not, he will shred and barbecue you. Anyway, a lot of people who should not have gotten arrested did. We were two of those unlucky ones. But I'd like to think that someone was watching over me when we wound up in the same cell. As different as we are, we are exactly the same." Chris snickers. "The one thing I stood up to my family about at Thanksgiving was not touching the turkey. You should have seen the look on Mom's face when I told her I went vegetarian. She actually called me a hippie!"

I've always known how lucky I am, but now it is driven home so hard that I feel it in the recesses of my gut. What would it have been like to grow up without support for my quirks? Would I have still become the person I am now, or would I be like Chris? A grown man who is struggling to find himself as if he were a teenager. He's not a bad boy, or a jerk, or a wannabe rebel. He's just a puppy learning to use his paws.

The last time I saw GranGran she asked me a question that now rings in my head. *What rebellion would you have gone through to find yourself?* I don't have an answer to that, because I never needed to rebel.

"What's your family like?" he asks.

It's sort of a trick question, because I am fortunate in that pretty much everyone in my life is like family. "My family are my friends, and my friends are family. Each and every one of them is everything that people like us need those in our lives to be."

Chris's eyes get misty, and he doesn't try to hide it. "Do you have any idea how lucky you are?"

The question strikes a chord that lays in the pit of my soul. I've always known I was blessed, but now I see my blessings through a new set of eyes. "I do now."

I have so many questions, but he is putting the past away, and he doesn't have all the answers yet about his future. During my age of discovery, the last thing I needed was people asking me the same questions I was asking myself. What I needed was for them to let me fall. Chris has more than earned that respect. He didn't have to level with me about so much, but I am grateful that he did. We are kindred spirits, and in seeing that, I feel my heart slip out of my chest and land on my sleeve—not because I am losing my defenses, but because I am growing stronger.

Suddenly my world seems magical. Now I notice music tinkling in the air. The snow-covered trees enrobe me in the scent of pine, and the mounds of snow that surround us remind me of marshmallows. My world has always been a wonderland. Now I appreciate it as such.

Chris leads me onto the ice. Naturally it is not long until I fall, but the challenge is a reminder that there is much in the world to discover. Besides, maybe in his seeing me fall, I can help Chris stand.

Super Sunny Christmas

This year, the day before Christmas Eve holds nearly as much excitement as the big day itself. I'm so psyched that I squeal when I grab my suitcase.

A squeal? Who am I? Rox? She squeals. I—I—

Well, I guess now I squeal too.

It seems silly that I have packed for a few days away when I am only headed across town to stay with my parents. Bailey comes home today, and we want to keep embracing the holidays with as many of the old traditions as we can. That includes falling asleep under the tree together on Christmas Eve while waiting for Santa to bring us our haul.

I lock my apartment door and start to head down the stairs, only to be blinded when I step out of the shade. The sun is so bright that I shy my head and then fumble through my purse in search of my sunglasses.

A pair of boots race up to meet me. My heart begins to sprint in hope, but my mind tells it to relax. The sun is too blinding for me to see who it is, but there is no way it could possibly be him.

I slip on my sunglasses and regain my vision enough to see Chris grab my bag. My words follow my gasp. "What are you doing here? I thought you were off to see your family?"

The sweetness of his kiss on my cheek isn't enough, so I tug him to race me down the stairs where we turn it into something much more romantic. I don't care why he is here, I am just glad that he is. I know he needs to get to the airport, so this will have to be brief. Damn, why haven't I mastered halting time? Or better yet, being in two places at once. Then we could stay in this state of bliss forever while still going on about our daily lives.

When we come up for air, he sounds as breathless as I feel. "I am so glad I caught you before you left."

Dear Lord, me too. I go in for another kiss.

Wait, he is talking about before *I* leave? The words were normal, but something about the implication sounded weird. "Is everything okay? Doesn't your flight leave any minute now?"

"Yes, and I am sure it will be happy to leave without me."

Without him? "Hey, I know you are not crazy about your family, but they are going to be heartbroken when you bail on Christmas."

"As soon as they get done screaming about how I have sold my soul to Satan, my family will be fine. Also, I'm not bailing on Christmas," he says, taking my hands. "I love Christmas, and that is exactly the reason why I will spend it talking to the one person we are all supposed to talk to on that day but rarely do. I'm headed up north to stare at snow-covered trees and find that part of me that has all the answers about who he is and what he wants to be. But first, I came to give you this."

Chris hands me a little box that is wrapped in gold paper and dabbed with a red bow. This is so sweet, but also so unfair. "Hey, you made a big deal out of saying no gifts."

"No, I made a big deal out of saying no *Christmas* gifts. Think of this as a thank you present."

"For what?" It's been weeks since our do-over date, and while we are, obviously, both glad that I gave him another chance, that was hardly gift worthy.

"For being who you are." He cups my cheeks with his hands, and everything about the moment—his tender yet insistent touch, the earnestness in his eyes, and the conviction in his voice—drives home a new reality. In a very short period of time, this man stopped flailing and found strength. How much it moves me shows in the water welling in my eyes. "When I'm with you," he says, "I don't think about who I am supposed to be, I just exist. I've found my relationship with myself. Now I need to find it with whoever is driving us all. That is why I am not at the airport."

All other amazing things aside, I'm so honored to be a part of his growth. Thank God GranGran intervened.

He brushes away my tears with his thumbs before kissing my forehead. "Go on. Open it," he whispers.

My emotions have me so dazed that all I can think to do is stare at the box and marvel at the gift I've been given—the gift of helping someone else find his way.

"Go on." He nudges my arm and winks. "I'm betting that you are someone who loves to rip into paper."

He already knows me so well that I am forced back into the moment. "Damn right I am." I start digging in.

Excitement rings in his voice like he is the one blessed with unexpected joy. "I found it on accident. I heard there was some stuff for the Vespa in an antique shop up the coast. That was a bust, but I did find this."

I open the box, and my hand flies to my mouth to cover my gasp. It's a pin—one that is the perfect match to the hair clips GranGran gave me. They could have been made from the same mold.

Oh, GranGran, I miss you so much. Though you are so far away, you are always right next to me. Chris finding this is your way of showing me that all is going exactly as it should. "Thank you," I utter to Chris while also holding GranGran in my heart.

His eyes lock into mine. "No, thank you for giving me that do-over. It kick started my life. Darla, I'd like to think I know what the future holds for us, but that is a fool's game. What I do know is that every day you give me more clay, more incentive, to shape myself. That is making me whole, and that is exactly how it should be."

He wishes me happiness and heads off with the promise of a perfect New Year's Eve ahead. I truly hope he finds what he is looking for. Something tells me that I have.

Getting In The Mood (For Christmas)

The swinging sounds of a big band waft through my parent's house while I put away the last glass from lunch. In the distance, Dad's laughter erupts. Ever since GranGran died all those years ago, Bailey and I have been on a mission to spice up the day. While we have created new traditions that bring joy, such as her Swing dancing with Dad, we've never been able to fill the void that losing GranGran put in our hearts.

As I pass the family room, I pause to look at the admiration in my father's eyes for his eldest daughter. The parent/child relationship is always a love story of its own. I hope to have several of those someday. I'm even allowing myself to think that maybe the first one will start sooner than anyone expects, even me. Love happens every day, and now it is finally happening to me.

Chris was mostly right with his reasoning for no gifts, but he forgot something key: he is a gift to me as well. Chris is a reminder of the wonderful people I have in my life and the support with which they have embraced me. When you are used to something, it is easy to lose sight of its importance.

Speaking of which, my own tradition is calling me. The most important person in the world waits in my room. She is also in my heart, my spirit, and in a photograph.

I grab GranGran's picture from where I set it on my old nightstand. Her eyes fill me with just as much love as if she were here. She will be soon.

As I head for my suitcase, azure haze slinks in front of me. My body tingles as if the arms of an angel have embraced me.

"Looking for someone?"

My breath locks when I turn and set my eyes on GranGran. "How did you get here? I haven't even pulled the board out of my suitcase."

GranGran nudges me to take a seat with her on the bed, just like we always did. "Do you really think a silly, little trinket connects us? Your heart is what holds the secret to being with me. For us, that board is insignificant. However, there is something very important that I need you to do with it."

Her eyes lock onto mine. As much as I have always seen her ghost as a person, I've also been aware that her image is composed of energy that appears as mist. But now, deep in the recesses of her eyes, I see something more. Is it a reflection? A light? A window into where she now lives? The glow of God?

Maybe it is my imagination, but for the life of me I sense something different in her voice. Her words are almost too clear, as if someone is speaking them for her. "That special planchette I gave you was the last thing I painted. Please, never let it go. However, the first chance you get, I want you to take that board and the plastic planchette it came with over to Rox. Don't actually give it to her. Just slip it into the closet along with her board games. She will find it when the time is right. What you have experienced with me may be sweet, but the adventure that awaits her is nothing short of fantastic."

Goosebumps coat my skin. Each one holds hope for the dreams of my friend. With GranGran behind the scenes, I can only begin to imagine where life can take us.

She double pats my knee. "I am so very proud of you. If you ever need me, just wish me here. Even if you don't see me, I will always be near. Goodbye, darling. I love you, and Merry Christmas."

"I love you, too."

GranGran's haze fades without leaving a physical trace. She may be gone from this earth, yet every day she creates beauty here because of the love she left behind. This year, that beauty taught me that Christmas isn't about opening presents; it is about opening our hearts. For that reason, and for some many others, Christmas itself, just like the love we share, is magic.

Joy To The World

Chris is barely inside my door before he sweeps me off my feet and flies me into a spin. His happiness is so powerful that it causes me to laugh with joy. "I sure missed you," he tells me.

As much as the newness of this relationship has me feeling the need to keep reality in check, a bigger part of me believes in admitting what I know to be true. "I missed you, too. Did you find what you were looking for?"

His stare into my eyes isn't one that sends waves of love through me. Instead, I sense him searching inside us both and questioning just how much he is ready to share. I get it. There is so much I want to tell him, but telling anyone about the daisies I follow is a long way off. I won't blame him in the least if he doesn't utter a word about his time away.

"Yeah," he says, setting me down. "I did find it. I'm not going to share it with people either, for reasons that will become obvious, but I'll show you."

"Please don't feel you need to explain anything about yourself to me."

"I don't, but I like you being in my life. I hope that someday you will see this anyway, but I'd rather just come out with it. With what I am learning about myself, being around me is tricky enough. If you can understand what I did then … Well, let me just show you." He removes his leather jacket. "This is going to be weird."

My heart skips a little. I like him being in my life, too. Did he really feel the need to warn me, of all people, about something being weird? What could he—

Chris unbuttons his shirt and pulls it open at the chest. I

can't help but let my eyes wander to every exposed piece of flesh. Dear lord of all that is firm and carved by heaven! I suspected it was decent under there but ...

Did the heater just come on? I could swear I turned it off.

Wait, what's up with the bandage over his heart?

As Chris pulls away the tape, the fact that he got a tattoo becomes apparent. It looks like an outline of a cross but ... Did someone drag an unloaded tattoo gun across him?

I step closer and see that the outline was done in white. Since it is still red around the edges, it doesn't look so much like a tattoo, but more like a brand from an iron that had only been warmed.

"I warned you that it was weird," he says.

"A cross isn't weird, but why so faint?"

"My wack job family got one thing right. They taught me to believe in something greater than myself. However, they would have gotten through to me a lot more if they had not shoved their beliefs down my throat. God wants us to be humble. Is telling someone that if he gets a tattoo, he will burn in hell, humble? No, it is saying you think you are better than they are because of your choices. I can't see how God would want that."

"So, you got a tattoo to show your family you know your own mind. Why is it so faint and put where they won't see it?" He starts to button his shirt. My eyes wish he wouldn't, but my mind is being held captive by his words.

"Faith is personal. I am the only one who needs to know that a mark of any kind is on my body. That cross is a part of me now, just like my faith always has been. If and when I decide there is something else I want on my body for the rest of my life, I'll have it put on how and where I feel it is best."

Chris takes back his jacket and puts it on before reaching to the sofa for my coat.

"So, do you think I wussed out?" he asks.

I snicker at my own memories of becoming self-aware. "No. I think you dyed your hair. On the way to Mulligan's, I'll tell you the story of the Christmas when Bailey bought me my first real makeup, and how it led to my glorious mane."

He runs his fingers through my hair. Though his look of admiration is aimed at my locks, the simple gesture steals my breath. He might as well be whisking me off to Heaven. "I love this about you. Why doesn't it surprise me that it wasn't done on a whim?"

God, that word. That big, scary, four-letter word that he used so freely regarding who I am. He doesn't weigh his thoughts nor does he measure his words, and that is one of the things that I love about him. "Everything that reflects who we are has a story behind it." Someday I hope to tell him the full version, but for now, I'll stick to the basics.

We head out to meet our friends, but not before detouring by Rox and Jacqueline's place. With the aid of the key they gave me for emergencies, I let myself inside, head down the hall to the family room, and open the closet door. The smell of musty records tickles my nose, but how that aroma is a fine bouquet to my comrade in quirks warms my heart.

"Rox, you and your affair with music is a grand love story all its own. Sonnets could be written about it."

I barely manage to slip Ouija between Monopoly and Risk. She'll probably think it is the same board we used at slumber parties when we were kids. Funny how it blends in as if it were just another game, yet it is anything but that. Then again, GranGran said I never truly needed it, so maybe it is just a game after all.

Faith is a funny thing. It makes what seems impossible real.

Goosebumps rise as I kiss my fingertips and touch them to the box one last time. How painful it is to say goodbye to cardboard surprises me; however, I find joy in knowing I will keep GranGran's love in my heart forever.

"Happy New Year, GranGran. I love you."

The slightest tingle floats across me, as if I am being smiled upon. Tears fill my eyes, because even though I don't hear her saying it, I know GranGran is telling me she loves me too. I blow a kiss toward Heaven before leaving the board behind.

Chris and I head off to Mulligan's, the place where we gather with friends and celebrate life. It is not the place that counts; it is the love everyone brings there.

Discover the future of the Ouija board with Rox, Jacqueline, and Darla in the novel *Scary Modsters … and Creepy Freaks.* Then follow Darla and Bailey into the companion novel, *Voices Carry,* available soon. These are all a part of *The Rock and Roll Fantasy Collection*—a set of stand-alone novels and novellas. The novels revolve around characters whose deep-seated love of music is a driving force of the story, while the novellas focus on the supporting characters that you can't help but love.

Playlist

"Parade Of The Wooden Soldiers" - The Crystals
"Christmas Wrapping" - The Waitresses
"Santa Claus Wants Some Lovin'" - Mack Rice
"Christmas Bop" - T. Rex
"Someday At Christmas" - Jackson Five
"It's A Marshmallow World" - Darlene Love
"Super Sunny Christmas" - Redd Kross
"Getting In The Mood (For Christmas)" - Brian Setzler Orchestra
"Joy To The World" - Chuck Negron

More by Diane Rinella

The Rock and Roll Fantasy Collection
Scary Modsters…and Creepy Freaks
Queen Midas in Reverse
Voices Carry
Moonlight Serenade

Something to Dream On

The Forbidden Flower Series
Love's Forbidden Flower
Time's Forbidden Flower

About the Author

Enjoying San Francisco as a backdrop, the ghosts in *USA Today* Bestselling Author Diane Rinella's 150-year old Victorian home augment the chorus in her head. With insomnia as their catalyst, these voices have become multifarious characters that haunt her well into the sun's crowning hours, refusing to let go until they have manipulated her into succumbing to their whims. Her experiences as an actress, business owner, artisan cake designer, software project manager, Internet radio disc jockey, vintage rock n' roll journalist/fan girl, and lover of dark and quirky personalities influence her idiosyncratic writing.

You can visit her website at www.dianerinellaauthor.com and on Facebook at https://www.facebook.com/DianeRinellaAuthor/